Contents

KT-377-123

Introduction

He looked slowly around the room. He had the feeling that something was wrong. In a strange place, he always checked everything before he went to bed. There was some movement under the sheets. Quickly he pulled the sheets back and saw a yellow-brown snake. It lifted its head and made dangerous sounds. It was ready to attack. Its bite could kill.

There's something wrong with the Blue Mines at Arralooma in Central Australia. Are they only mining opals there, or are they doing other things? The Australian police are worried. The police in other countries are, too. When a young policeman is found dead not far from the Blue Mines, the Special Police Team in Sydney sends up one of their best men, Steve Malone.

Arralooma is a small place, hot and dry. Most of the miners live underground. Steve wants to learn more about the Blue Mines, but it isn't easy. Nobody wants to talk. He makes some friends in Arralooma. But he soon realizes that he also has dangerous enemies. They are trying to kill him before he learns too much. Can he complete his job before they succeed?

Kris Anderson was a university teacher and worked on a dictionary, *The Longman Dictionary for Language Teaching and Applied Linguists* (1985, 1992). Now she is a writer. Many of her books are for learners of English; for example, *Better Ways with Adjectives and Adverbs* (1992), *Better Ways with Nouns and Pronouns* (1993), *Better Ways with Phrasal Verbs* (1995). She also writes detective stories and love stories for young people.

Chapter 1 Death in the Blue Mines

Andy McLeod was running as fast as he could. It didn't help. The thick white fog was coming closer. Andy was breathing with difficulty. The tunnel was getting darker and narrower. Suddenly, his hands touched a hard rock wall in front of him. The end of the tunnel! He screamed. He couldn't continue. And the white fog was now all around him. He couldn't breathe. It filled his nose and his mouth. Suddenly, a terrible pain went through his body.

e fell to his knees. As he fell onto the wet floor of the tunnel, he pulled the little recorder from his belt. 'Andy McLeod,' he spoke into it with difficulty, 'died at Arralooma – job completed.'

♦

Two Days Later – in Sydney . . .

It was one of those hot, bright days in Sydney. The sky was light blue and cloudless. Steve Malone stopped his red car in front of a narrow house. It was in a quiet side street in an older part of the city. The house looked like the others in the street, simple and white. A small metal sign near the front door read 'S. P. Brown Electronics'.

Steve smiled. There was no S. P. Brown Electronics. Inside the building were the offices of a special police team. The people in the team were used by the Australian government for difficult and often dangerous work.

'Is the boss in?' Steve asked the young man at the front desk.

'Is he in?' The man laughed. 'That's a joke! He's in and he's already asked for you ten times. He's not very happy, I can tell you.'

Steve laughed. 'That's not unusual.' He walked through a room filled with boxes to a lift.

'Number?' a deep male voice asked.

Steve spoke his number into a microphone near the lift door. The door opened and he stepped inside. The lift stopped at the next floor. A metal door opened and Steve stepped into a large room.

The short, grey-haired man behind the dark wooden desk looked angrily at Steve. 'Where have you been?' he asked. 'I've left messages for you.'

'On the beach. The weather's beautiful. Remember – I'm on holiday.'

'Not now,' the man told him. 'I need you immediately. [illegible] have to go up to Arralooma, the opal mining place. We ha[illegible] problems up there. One of the miners was killed.'

'Why does that interest us?' Steve asked, surprised. 'That's a matter for the police there.'

'The miner was one of our men – Andy McLeod.'

'Andy!' Steve felt cold inside. Andy was a special friend. They often worked together. He tried to remember Andy's smiling young face, his laugh. He closed his eyes.

Steve's boss didn't speak. He looked at the tall, strong young man with the handsome face. 'An excellent man, Steve Malone,' he thought. 'He's fearless and intelligent but he has feelings. It's good that way – he's not just a machine.'

Steve looked up. His face was suddenly hard. 'Give me the story,' he said.

'It's like this. An international company, Blue Mines, owns a large opal mine in Arralooma. We've got information about them from the police in other countries. Blue Mines don't just mine opals. They're doing strange things, but we don't know enough about them. The Australian government is getting very worried. They want action – fast! The local police searched the mine and found nothing wrong. So we sent Andy up to Arralooma.'

'Who's the boss up there?' Steve asked.

'They have a manager. He's called Duvall. The police in a number of countries would like to talk to him. But there's also a scientist at the mine. That's very strange. There's never a scientist at an opal mine. Most of the workers come from other countries, but there are a few Australians.'

'When did Andy go to Arralooma?' Steve asked.

'Last month.'

'And did he learn anything?'

'Yes, that's what's so terrible. We got a secret message from him.

It said: "Things are going well and I'm going in." I think he meant "into the mine". Then he was found – dead!'

'Where?' Steve asked quickly.

'Near an old mine shaft. It belongs to the McKenzie Mine. It's not used now. People say the ghosts of dead men walk there at night.'

'Is the McKenzie Mine near the Blue Mines' place?'

'Not far from it, but not on their land.'

'Who found Andy's body?' Steve asked.

'An old Aborigine called Moornie. He owns a small mine near the McKenzie Mine. Moornie found Andy early in the morning. Andy was lying with his face down on the ground near the mine shaft. He was dead. His face looked terrible. He died in great pain.'

'How did he die?'

'We don't know yet. We don't think he was killed with a gun or a knife. But we'll know soon.'

'How?' Steve asked.

The man opposite gave him a thin smile. 'You're going to discover that for us, Steve. We'll fly you up to Arralooma tomorrow. You're a writer for a travel magazine and your name is Steve Carter. Here are your papers – a driver's licence and a licence to carry a gun. Good luck!'

Chapter 2 Arrival at Arralooma

A special plane landed Steve at a lonely place about seventy kilometres south of Arralooma. Two men were waiting for him there.

'There's your car.' One of them pointed to an old green Land Rover. 'You'll get to Arralooma by this evening, if you start immediately.'

'Thanks.' Steve threw his two bags into the back of the Land Rover and drove off. The road was terrible. It was narrow and sandy and in some parts full of small rocks. On both sides of the road there were low, flat-topped hills, a few trees and grey-green grasses.

It was very hot. The bright light of the sun made Steve's eyes ache. His shirt was sticking to his back. He felt uncomfortable. When he finally arrived in Arralooma, he was tired, hot and dirty.

Arralooma was a strange place. It was very hot during the day and most of the miners didn't live in houses above the ground. They made very large holes in the sides of the low hills. The front of each hole was then closed up with wood. It had a door and sometimes one or two windows. These places were called dugouts. Some dugouts were very comfortable inside.

There were only a few buildings above ground – a police station, a pub, a small hospital and a large shop with a post office. Steve couldn't see any gardens, just sandy earth with stones and a few grasses.

Steve drove to the pub. It was a larger building than the others. He could hear shouting and laughter from inside the building. The main room was large. The bar was at one end. The room was crowded with men in jeans and T-shirts. Some had beards and long hair.

Steve pushed through them to the bar. A young woman was pouring out beer. She was wearing a close-fitting green top and jeans. Her long black hair was tied back. She turned and smiled at Steve. He noticed that she had large green eyes. 'Like a cat,' Steve thought, 'a beautiful cat.'

'Hi!' He rested one arm on the bar. 'I'm Steve Carter, the travel magazine writer. I rang from Sydney.'

'Hi, Steve.' She looked at him and smiled. 'I'm Sheila. My dad owns the pub. So you got here all right. Your room's ready. It's at the back. Go outside, turn right and right again. Third door along. The key's in the door. Where are your things?'

'In the car.'

'Leave them there. Come and join the others. They're a nice crowd – a bit rough sometimes. Dave had good luck today. He found a large opal in his mine. He's paying for the drinks. Do you want a beer?'

'Fine. What about some food, Sheila?'

'Steak and eggs - okay? I'll bring it to you when it's ready.'

Steve tried to push his way through the crowd to one of the rough wooden tables. He noticed a group of men standing at one end of the bar. There were four of them, dressed like miners. Steve could sense that they were different. They looked unpleasant. He felt uncomfortable. Who were they? Blue Mines workers? One of them, a big man, was trying to push a young Aborigine away from the bar.

'Leave Eddie alone!' Sheila screamed at him – but it was too late. The man pushed Eddie over. The young Aborigine was on the floor. His beer glass was broken and beer was everywhere. The man was lifting his foot to give Eddie a kick. Steve jumped at him. A second later, the man was lying on the floor, screaming with pain. His three friends were moving towards Steve, ready to attack. Steve saw that the other miners were moving back. Nobody wanted to help him. Okay, he could fight alone. It was difficult. They probably had knives. Steve moved one step back – he was prepared.

There was a shout from the back of the room. A very large man with red hair pushed his way through the crowd.

'No fights in my pub!' he shouted. 'You started it, Max!' He pulled the man to his feet. 'Get out! And take your friends with you!'

They did as they were told. Max moved towards the door and the others followed him. Max gave Steve an unpleasant look as he went out.

'You be careful with those men!' Sheila put the plate with steak and eggs and a large piece of bread in front of Steve. 'They're from the Blue Mines – very dangerous! It's not a good idea to fight them!'

Steve laughed. 'I like fighting.'

She looked at the strong young man in front of her. 'And I can see you're good at it, Steve,' she said with a smile.

Steve looked around for Eddie, the young Aborigine, but Eddie was gone. The other miners started to leave. Steve suddenly felt very tired. The steak was too salty and the eggs too dry. He finished his beer and walked outside.

It was dark now and it was getting cooler. Steve drove the Land Rover round to the back of the pub. There was a walkway with a wooden floor all the way along the building. Steve noticed five doors and next to each one a narrow window. 'Probably all bedrooms,' he thought. He parked the Land Rover in front of the third door and got his bags out.

The key was large and probably fitted other doors. Steve switched on the light. His room was small, with little furniture in it. There was a cupboard, a table and two old wooden chairs. The bed in the corner was covered by two dirty grey sheets. 'Not exactly comfortable,' Steve thought, 'but good enough.'

He looked slowly around the room. He had the feeling that something was wrong. In a strange place, he always checked everything before he went to bed. There was some movement under the sheets. Quickly he pulled the sheets back and saw a yellow-brown snake. It lifted its head and made dangerous sounds. It was ready to attack. Its bite could kill.

Steve took a chair and crashed it down on the snake's head. The snake moved quickly around the leg of the chair. Steve ran outside and hit the chair on the ground. The leg broke and the snake disappeared into the darkness.

Steve looked along the back of the building. All was quiet. He walked along and looked into the other four windows, but everything was dark. He went back into his room and searched every corner of it. Finally, he pushed the other chair against the door and lay down on the bed. He felt angry. The snake wasn't in his bed by accident. Somebody knew why he was here. They were prepared for him! 'It's going to be a difficult job,' he thought.

Chapter 3 The Secret Airfield

When Steve woke up in the morning, there was bright sunshine outside. He heard a knock at the window and saw a dark face.

'Eddie!' Steve jumped up and pulled on his jeans. The face disappeared. Steve pushed the chair away and opened the door. Eddie was standing at the back of the building, looking at the sandy ground.

'You had a fight with a snake,' he said, and pointed to the broken chair. 'It got away.'

'Yeah. I found it last night in my bed, under the sheets.'

Eddie shook his head. 'Those snakes like warm places. Was the door open?'

'No. But the key was in the door.'

'It was a yellow-brown snake,' Eddie said.

'It was. How do you know?'

'I can see.' Eddie pointed to the ground. He moved his hand, showing the movements of a snake. 'Very dangerous. One bite can kill you.' He looked again at Steve. 'Someone hates you,' he said slowly. 'You be careful.'

'I will. You can be sure of that,' Steve told him.

Eddie kicked the sandy ground with his foot. 'My uncle Moornie wants to meet you,' he told Steve. 'Want to come with me now?'

Steve was pleased. Moornie was the old Aborigine who found Andy's body. There were many things he wanted to ask him. 'Yeah. I can come now.' He didn't want breakfast. He still remembered the salty steak. 'Have you got a car, Eddie? Or do we take mine?'

'You take your car. Turn right behind the shop. Drive along the road a short way and wait for me.' Eddie walked along the back of the hotel and disappeared.

♦

Steve didn't have to wait long on the sandy road. An old yellow car drove very fast past him, sending up clouds of sand. Eddie was driving. He waved to Steve. Steve followed the car. 'Eddie doesn't want to drive with me,' Steve thought. 'Why? And he hasn't thanked me for my help with Max. But he's invited me to see his uncle. Maybe that's his way of saying "Thank you".'

They had to drive quite a long way along the narrow, sandy road. There were no trees or houses, only grey-green grass here and there and a few rocks. Steve could see some low hills farther away, and some metal posts and a few cars. 'Those are probably opal mines,' he thought.

Suddenly, Eddie turned his car to the left and drove over the sandy ground to a small, low hill. Steve could see that part of it was a miner's dugout. The front was covered with wood and there was a door in it, and a window next to that. Behind the hill were large piles of sand and a big hole. It looked like the entrance to a mine.

Eddie jumped out of his car. He pulled the door to the dugout open and called out something in an Aboriginal language. An old man came out to greet Steve. He had a round brown face, white hair and a short white beard. Moornie stood and looked at Steve for a long time. There was understanding in those dark eyes.

'He knows who I am. He knows why I'm here.' Steve began to get worried. 'I must be careful how I ask him about Andy.'

Suddenly Moornie smiled, stepped back and invited Steve into the dugout. It was quite large. It was built into the hill and the walls were rock. Some parts were covered with wood. The front part of the dugout was the living area with an old sofa, a large table and chairs. There were two rooms off the main area. One was a bedroom, the other a kitchen. Eddie boiled some water on a gas ring and made strong, sweet tea.

'I'm writing for a travel magazine,' Steve told Moornie. 'I want to write about Arralooma. About things that happen here, everyday things, unusual things. You found a dead man near your mine, is that right?'

The old man shook his head. 'Not near my mine. Near the McKenzie Mine.'

'But that's not very far from here?'

'No – over there.' Moornie pointed towards the north. 'Found him in the morning. He was dead – dead for many hours.'

'Someone killed him?'

'Yeah.' There was a strange smile on the old man's face.

'Do you know who?' Steve asked quickly.

'Yeah. McKenzie's ghost. That man had fear on his face, terrible fear. McKenzie killed him.' Moornie spoke slowly. 'He doesn't want anyone in his mine. He guards his mine.'

'Tell him, Uncle,' Eddie said. 'Tell Steve about the McKenzies!'

And the old man told the story of the two McKenzie brothers, Billy and Robert. 'They were always fighting. And they didn't find many opals. Only a few small ones. One day, Robert was making a new tunnel. Billy wanted to stop him. They started to fight again and Robert took his gun and shot Billy. Robert disappeared. Later they found him. He killed himself. But he cannot rest. His ghost walks about, protecting the mine.'

'Why?' Steve asked.

'Ah,' Eddie said. 'Some people say there are still big opals in that mine.'

The old man shook his head. 'And some say there aren't. You don't believe in ghosts, writer?'

'No, I don't.'

The old man smiled. 'Then you tell me how that man died.'

'I don't know.' Steve couldn't understand why Andy's little cassette recorder wasn't found. 'You didn't find anything on the dead man, did you, Moornie? Something that can explain his death?'

'No.' Again the strange smile.

Steve realized that Moornie was keeping quiet about something. 'What do the other miners think about it?' he asked.

'I don't know, writer.' The old man shook his head. 'I don't ask questions. It's not good to ask too many questions. It's dangerous. Maybe you should remember that.'

'The old Aborigine knows a lot more,' Steve thought, 'but he isn't going to tell me – not now.' He wanted to get up and leave. But then he heard a car outside.

'Hey, anybody at home?' a loud voice called out, and the door was pushed open. A thin, fair-haired man stepped inside. He wore only a dirty T-shirt and a pair of jeans. Steve could see that he had pictures of birds on both his arms.

The man stopped and looked angrily at Steve. 'Who's he?' he asked.

'That's Steve,' Eddie told him. 'He helped me against Big Max. He hit Big Max.'

'That's great!' The man shook Steve's hand. 'Eddie's friend is *my* friend. And I'm pleased to be the friend of a man who's hit Big Max. I'm Jim Bowman, I work at the Blue Mines. What about you? Are you a miner? You don't look like one.'

'No,' Steve told him, 'I'm a writer. I'm writing about Arralooma and the mines here. What about the Blue Mines? There's been a bit of talk. Do they only mine opals?'

Jim shook his head. 'Sorry, Steve. I'm not talking. They pay me well. I was in prison in Adelaide. When I got out, I couldn't get a job. Then these Blue Mines people found me. And they gave me a job – no questions asked. So you see, I'm not talking.'

'But you don't like Big Max?'

'No, I don't – and I don't like the manager and that strange friend of his, that Dr Frank. But I keep my ears closed and I look the other way. So I can't help you. Sorry, Steve.'

'Okay.' Steve got up. 'I must go now. Thanks for the tea, Moornie. See you later, Eddie.'

'Can you find your way back?' Jim asked.

'I think so.' Steve went outside. He noticed with surprise that Eddie followed him.

As Steve was getting into his car, Eddie opened the door. He got in next to Steve. 'I want to show you something,' he said.

When they reached the road, Eddie told Steve to turn left, not right. They drove for a few kilometres. The road became narrower and narrower. Finally, it came to an end. They drove across a sandy, rocky plain.

Suddenly, Eddie told Steve to stop the car. He jumped out and walked quickly onto a flat piece of land. Steve followed. He noticed lines in the ground, made by wheels. He realized that the lines were wide, very wide, too wide for cars. A plane! Planes were landing here! He suddenly realized that he was standing in the middle of an airfield. A secret airfield. The Blue Mines! Was it for the Blue Mines?

'Listen, Eddie.' Steve turned round – but he couldn't see Eddie. He called out, but nobody answered. He walked quickly back to his car. Maybe Eddie was sitting in the car? But the car was empty. Steve looked back along the road. Far away, he could see the young Aborigine. Eddie was running along at a great speed. Soon he disappeared. Steve was pleased to know about the airfield. But now he wanted to ask questions about it.

Steve remembered Moornie's words: 'It's dangerous to ask too many questions.' Well, he had to ask questions and he had to get answers – fast. He decided to visit the Blue Mines.

Chapter 4 A Visit to the Blue Mines

The entrance to the Blue Mines was on a narrow road off the road from Pimboola to Arralooma. The Blue Mines' land had a tall metal fence around it. Steve thought that it was probably an electric fence. There was a wide gate and next to it a narrow door. Behind the door was a small wooden building for a guard. It had windows all around it. Steve tried the narrow metal door. It opened. He walked through to the guard's building.

'Yeah? What do you want?' The man in the guard's building had short fair hair and a large red face. Steve remembered him. He was one of Big Max's friends. Steve was sure that the man remembered him too.

'I'm Steve Carter!' Steve tried to sound friendly. 'I'm writing a story about Arralooma and the mines. I'd like to have a talk to your manager.'

'No hope! Our manager doesn't want to talk to people like you.' The man's little eyes were full of hate.

'How do you know?' Steve asked. 'Why don't you ask him?'

'Can't.' The man laughed loudly. 'He isn't in. And we don't want you here – at any time, you understand?'

'Why not?' Steve asked.

'Because I don't like you,' the man shouted at him. 'That's why. And Big Max doesn't like you either. Get off our land fast or you'll be sorry! I'll teach you a lesson you won't forget quickly.' He pulled a gun from his pocket.

Steve smiled at him. 'I don't like you either,' he said slowly. Then he turned around and walked out again by the narrow door. He breathed more freely when he reached his car. He didn't like to walk with a gun in his back. But the Blue Mines people wouldn't like to have another murder on their hands – not just now.

He looked across to the main buildings. There were four of

them. Two looked like houses for the manager and his friend. The third one was bigger. Maybe the miners slept there. The fourth building was a little way away from the others. It was made of wood and looked tall and narrow. Steve guessed that it was the entrance to the mine shaft.

'Why do they have a building over the shaft?' he thought. Most opal mines didn't cover their shaft. He wanted so much to get there and have a look. It was stupid to try now. At night, then. 'I can cut through the metal fence,' he thought. 'Maybe at the bottom of the fence. Or maybe I can push myself under the fence.' He had a good look around. He noticed a place to the left of the gate where it was possible. From there it wasn't very far to the entrance of the mine shaft.

Suddenly, Steve heard the sound of a car. A large grey Mercedes came along the sandy road and stopped in front of the gate. There were two men in it. The driver was a good-looking, dark-haired man of about forty. The guard came out of his building and started to open the gate. So they weren't visitors; they worked at the mine.

Steve went up to the car.

'Mr Duvall?' he asked.

'Yes.' The man looked at him in surprise.

'I'm Steve Carter. I'm writing about Arralooma for a magazine. I'd like to say something about your mine. It's the biggest mine in the area. Can I talk to you about it?'

Duvall smiled. His smile didn't look very friendly. 'Sorry, Mr Carter. I'm a very busy man. I really haven't got the time.'

'It won't take long, Mr Duvall. If you're too busy today, I can come back tomorrow.'

The same unfriendly smile. 'Sorry, Mr Carter. I'm too busy. Talk to the owners of the smaller mines. They always like to talk to someone.'

Steve had a good look at the other man in the car. He was

older than Duvall and had short white hair. But his face was strange. It was very pale, nearly white. The man's eyes were pink. And they were hard – as hard as metal. 'He looks like a ghost,' Steve thought.

The gate was now open. The white-haired man turned to Duvall. 'Let's go!' he ordered. Duvall did as he was told. The grey Mercedes moved off in a cloud of sand.

'Who gives the orders at the mine,' Steve asked himself. 'Mr Duvall or the stranger? Is he that scientist, Dr Frank? What kind of scientist is Dr Frank? Why do they need a scientist at an opal mine?'

Steve remembered the secret airfield. It wasn't necessary to fly out opals. Opals were small. A small lorry could take them to Pimboola and from there they could send them to Adelaide. No, Steve was sure that Blue Mines were mining something heavier than opals, bigger than opals. And they had to fly it out secretly, by plane. But what? 'I've studied maps of the area,' Steve thought. 'I talked to some scientists before I flew to Arralooma. Nobody has been able to give me an answer.'

He shook his head and got into his car. He couldn't do anything before dark.

♦

Near the Pimboola road, he realized that somebody was following him. A big car was coming after him, driving very fast. He could see the driver. It was Big Max. But Max wasn't alone. Two other men were sitting next to him. Maybe there were more in the back of the car. Steve suddenly felt cold inside. He couldn't see their faces very well, but he could hear them shouting. He tried to drive faster but the wheels of his car moved around in the sand.

He had to slow down again. The other car was close behind him. Now it was next to him. It turned left and pushed Steve's car to the side of the road. There was a sharp noise of metal against metal.

Steve stopped the car fast and threw himself to the left. Just in time. He heard a shot as a bullet went over his head. He pulled his gun from his pocket. 'Don't shoot, Max!' he heard a voice calling. 'Get him out of the car first. We want to have some fun. Let's teach him a lesson.'

Quickly Steve pushed open the left-hand door and jumped out. Somebody opened the right-hand door and Steve could hear angry shouts. Steve jumped in front of the car and pointed his gun straight at Big Max. 'I've got you, Max!' His voice was hard. 'One move by you or one of your friends and you're dead!'

There were four of them – Big Max and three others. They stood only a few metres away from Steve, looking at him with

hate in their eyes. He wasn't sure how long he could keep them there. They looked like big wild animals, ready to attack him.

Suddenly, a car stopped behind them – a police car. 'What's happening here?' A man got out. He was tall and had a dark moustache.

Big Max turned to him. 'Just having a bit of fun with my friends, Sergeant.'

'Fun!' The man looked angrily at the two cars. 'Do you call that fun, pushing a car off the road? Get your car out of my way, Max! And what about you?' he said, turning to Steve. 'What are you doing with that gun? Have you got a licence for that thing?'

'Yes,' Steve said, and put the gun back in his pocket.

'Then I want to see it.' he shouted at Steve. 'Not here. At the police station. Who are you? We don't like strangers around here.

Not when they're waving their guns about. Do we?' he addressed the people from the Blue Mines.

'That's right, Sergeant,' said one of Max's friends with a loud laugh.

'What are you waiting for?' The sergeant turned again to Steve. 'I haven't got all day to wait for you. Get in your car and follow me. And give me that gun!' He held out his hand.

Steve gave him the gun. As he was driving after the sergeant's car to the Arralooma police station, he was angry with himself. Why didn't he guess that Duvall's men were coming after him? And now he had to explain to this policeman what he was really doing in Arralooma. That was the one thing that he didn't want to do!

Chapter 5 Bill Travers

Steve sat opposite the sergeant in the small office of the Arralooma police station. The man introduced himself as Sergeant Bill Travers. Steve introduced himself as Steve Carter, a travel writer for a magazine.

'What's Sergeant Travers like? Is he a friend or an enemy?' Steve thought. 'He saved me from Big Max, but he hasn't been very pleasant since then. Now he has my gun.'

The sergeant was looking at Steve's driver's licence and his licence to carry a gun. They were both in the name of Steve Carter.

'Why is he taking so long?' Steve was getting impatient.

Suddenly, Travers looked up with a smile. 'They're very good, Mr Malone,' he said. 'They look like real licences.'

Steve's heart jumped. 'What do you mean?' He tried to stay calm.

'I mean your people are very good at making these licences.'

Steve looked at the man. 'Friend or enemy?' he asked himself again.

Sergeant Travers smiled at him. 'You can trust me, you know. It's sad that Andy didn't trust me. He needed my help.'

'What do you know?' Steve asked in a hard voice.

'Well, first, I realized that something was wrong with the Blue Mines people. The Pimboola police did, too. They went into the place, called it a check of the shaft and the tunnels. They searched and searched. But they didn't find anything! It was just a large opal mine. Then Andy arrived and started to ask questions. He was working at Pete's mine while Pete was in hospital. Something didn't seem quite right to me. And when Andy was found dead, I was sure. Andy was one of your men, and the Blue Mines people killed him.'

'How do you know about us, Bill?' Steve asked.

'I know someone in your team. We were good friends some time ago. I won't tell you his name. I rang him and told him about Andy's death. I offered to help. He was angry. "It's none of your business," he said, and put the phone down. But after that, I got a secret message. "Steve Malone is coming up to Arralooma," it said.'

'He was wrong to tell you.' Steve was angry.

'Probably – but I was able to help you today. Now what do you want to know about the Blue Mines?'

'What's wrong with the Blue Mines?'

'I'm not sure. Perhaps they aren't mining. Perhaps they're making something underground. If they're doing that, everything is well hidden.'

'I think it's something heavy, and a lot of it,' Steve said. He told Travers about the secret airfield.

'An airfield! I haven't found one and I've been all over the area. Where is it?'

'I can't tell you,' Steve said. 'I got lost when I tried to get back to the road. I was driving around in circles for hours. But Eddie knows.'

'Eddie won't tell me. He doesn't like the police.'

'He likes me,' Steve told him, 'because I hit Big Max. Maybe *you* should hit Big Max.'

Travers laughed. 'I don't think that's a good idea. I try not to fight with the Blue Mines people. And I try to look a bit stupid. It's easier for me to watch them. They think, "Stupid old Bill Travers – we don't have to worry about him!"'

Steve realized that Travers was a useful friend. 'Did you search Andy's body?' he asked.

'Yes, I did. Moornie found him, you know. He stayed with the body and sent Eddie to get me. What's missing?'

'Andy's little cassette recorder. It was usually hidden under his belt. I'm sure Andy has recorded something on the cassette. Moornie didn't find anything – he says.'

'Then they've got it,' Travers said.

'That's what I fear.' Steve looked angry. 'Maybe he used our secret language when he was speaking into the recorder – and maybe not. If he didn't, the Blue Mines people know all about Andy's job by now. Did you search the McKenzie Mine?'

'Yeah, I went down the shaft. But I couldn't go very far into the mine. The main tunnel was closed. The wooden posts have broken and a lot of sand has fallen in. I just couldn't get through.'

'Moornie thinks McKenzie's ghost killed Andy,' Steve told Travers.

'Don't believe it!' Travers looked angry. 'I'm sure he was killed by the Blue Mines people in some terrible way. His face showed that he was in great pain. And I'm sure that somebody told the Blue Mines people about Andy. Somebody who Andy trusted.'

Steve looked up in surprise. 'Any idea who?'

'I'm not sure – maybe Crazy Fred Vickers.'

'Who's he?'

'He owns the shop and he's one of the owners of the pub. I think he's a bit strange. And the Blue Mines people are good customers. They buy a lot in his shop. I don't trust him.'

'But Andy trusted him?'

'I think so. He was always talking to Fred. And then, of course, there's Liza, Andy's girlfriend.'

'Andy's girlfriend? I didn't know he had one.'

'Well, maybe she wasn't. But I often saw them talking together. And she only came to Arralooma last month. She works as an

opal cutter. They tell me she's very good at her work. She lives in one of the dugouts near the Pimboola road, not far from the Blue Mines turning. Maybe you should visit Fred and Liza.'

'Good idea!' Steve got up. 'Thanks, Bill, for your help.'

'Be careful, Steve!' Travers pushed Steve's gun across the desk. 'Don't forget this. I think you'll need it!'

Chapter 6 At Crazy Fred's Shop

Crazy Fred was a busy little man. When Steve went into the shop, Fred was pulling tins of vegetables out of a big box. He ran to Steve. 'Ah, you're the magazine writer, Steve Carter. Don't ask me how I know. I know everything that happens in Arralooma. Well, not much happens here, haha! You'll find a lot of things in my shop, Steve. And if you don't find anything, just tell me. I'll get it for you. Right?'

'Right.' Steve smiled at the little man. 'You're very busy here?'

'Always busy, Steve, always busy. Lots of customers.'

Steve looked around. The shop was empty. He couldn't see another person. 'But there's nobody here now,' he told Fred.

'Ah, not during the week. Not during the week, Steve. They're all down in the mines. But on Saturdays – you should see the shop on Saturdays. Crowds and crowds everywhere. They all buy from Crazy Fred. That's what they call me, haha!' The little man laughed, showing big white teeth. 'And I'm modern, very modern, Steve. Come and see my freezer. In this heat here, you need a large freezer. All the meat is there. And I get some vegetables from Pimboola. And there's room for other things too, haha. Very low temperature. Come and have a look! It's very modern. Like a big room. You just walk in.'

Fred opened a large door at the back of the shop. 'Come in! Have a look!' Fred took a step into the freezer. When Steve stepped in too, Fred suddenly jumped back. He tried to close the door, leaving Steve inside the freezer.

Steve threw himself back, and the large door shut with a loud noise only centimetres in front of his face. Angrily he turned round. 'Why did you do that?' he shouted at the little man.

Fred didn't answer. He was standing by the wall next to the freezer and was laughing loudly. His mouth, with the large white teeth, was wide open.

Steve went to the man and shook him. 'Stop laughing! I don't think that's funny. You wanted to kill me – a man can freeze to death in there!'

'It was a joke–' Fred was still laughing. 'Just a joke! You're clever, Steve, very clever. How did you guess what I wanted to do?'

'I don't trust anyone,' Steve said coldly.

'Oh, but you must trust Crazy Fred!' the man told him. 'I want to be your friend, Steve.'

'Well, you've got a funny way of showing it.'

'Fred!' Someone spoke from the front of the shop. 'Did you get that special coffee for me from Adelaide?'

'It's just arrived, Liza. Wait a minute, I'll get it for you.' Fred ran off to the back of the shop.

Steve turned round. 'She's one of the most interesting women I've ever seen,' he thought. Her long fair hair was pulled back from her face. It was a beautiful face with intelligent grey eyes. They were looking straight at Steve.

'Hi!' Steve smiled. 'I'm Steve Carter. Pleased to meet you.'

'Why?' Her voice was cold.

Steve knew the game. 'Because there aren't many women at Arralooma,' he said quickly.

'And any woman is better than no woman,' she answered back.

'That's right.'

'Sorry, Mr Carter, but I'm not interested. I'm very busy.' She

turned round and started to talk to Fred. She took out a shopping list and Fred put a number of things into a box for her. After she paid Fred, Steve moved towards her and took the box.

'Hey, what are you doing?' She sounded angry.

'I'm going to carry it to the car for you, Liza.' Steve smiled at her. 'I don't want money for the job.'

'Really?'

'Of course, you can invite me for a drink. Maybe a cup of that special coffee from Adelaide.'

She laughed. 'Okay, Steve, you win. One cup of coffee then. Follow me.' They left the shop together. Steve turned round. Crazy Fred was looking after them. Steve was sure that Fred looked angry. 'Why is he angry,' he asked himself.

♦

Liza's dugout was smaller than Moornie's, but with nice furniture. One part of the living area was a work place, another part was a small kitchen. There was an opening at the back to a bedroom. The place looked lovely. There was even a small flowering plant in a pot on the table, and there were a few pictures on the walls.

'A nice dugout. Is it yours?' Steve asked.

'No, it belongs to a friend,' Liza told him. 'He's lent it to me for a few months.'

Steve sat down in a small armchair. Liza boiled some water. She was wearing jeans and a white T-shirt. Her skin was light brown from the sun. Steve watched her. He enjoyed watching her.

He heard a car. It stopped outside the dugout. There was a knock on the door. Liza put her head outside and talked softly to someone. Steve could hear that she wasn't very pleased. She turned back to Steve. 'Sorry, Steve, I have to leave you alone for a few minutes. Make yourself some coffee when the water boils. I won't be long.' She went outside and shut the door behind her.

Steve went to the narrow window and looked out. A grey Mercedes was parked not very far away from Liza's dugout. And next to it stood Liza. She was talking to Duvall, the manager of the Blue Mines! He had his hand on her shoulder and she was smiling at him.

'So Duvall is Liza's friend,' Steve thought angrily. That was interesting!

He moved around the dugout and made a quick search. He

looked everywhere and into everything, in the living area and the small bedroom. Now and then he looked out of the window, but the two were still talking. Steve found what he was looking for. It was in the cupboard behind Liza's clothes. It was Andy's cassette recorder! But it was empty. The little cassette wasn't there!

Steve looked angrily at the cassette recorder. So Liza knew something about Andy's death.

'I liked Liza,' Steve thought sadly, 'I liked her a lot – but not now!'

He put the recorder back in the cupboard and started to make himself a cup of coffee. When Liza came back into the dugout, Steve was sitting at the table, slowly drinking his coffee. He smiled at her, but he was suddenly feeling very unhappy.

Chapter 7 Danger at the Blue Mines

Steve had his dinner at one of the tables in the hotel bar. He drank a glass of beer to wash down the salty taste from the steak. The room was crowded. Big Max was standing at the bar with some of his friends. Max didn't look at Steve. Steve noticed that none of the miners came to his table. They all seemed to be afraid of Max and his men.

When it was getting dark, Steve went out to his car. He carried one of his bags to his room. He always locked both his bags into the car now. He felt it was safer that way.

He took a few things from the bag, locked the door and turned off the light. He dressed in a black shirt and black jeans, put bullets in his gun and put it in his pocket. Then he sat down in one of the chairs and waited. He could hear the voices of the miners as they left the hotel. Finally, it was quiet.

Steve waited another half hour. Then he slowly opened the

door and looked outside. There was nobody there. His car was parked at the corner of the hotel. He drove off without lights. He only switched them on when he was away from the building. He couldn't see any other cars. Everyone in Arralooma seemed to be in bed.

♦

On the Pimboola road, he found the turning to the Blue Mines. He drove slowly and kept the lights of the car low. He stopped the car about a hundred metres from the Blue Mines, fence. Everything was in darkness. They didn't have any lights around the fence and near the gate, and he was pleased about that. It was easier this way.

Steve took a tool out of a secret box at the back of the car. Then he went to the fence. He hoped he could take out enough sand from below the fence. Then he could push himself through.

The sand was easy to move. Soon there was a big enough opening. Steve pulled a small black bag over his head to protect his hair and his face from the sand. It had holes for his eyes and his mouth. Then he pushed himself slowly through the opening onto the Blue Mines' land.

The top part of his body was through the opening, when he suddenly heard loud, heavy breathing. It came closer. Steve could hear the sound of small feet, moving faster and faster. He pushed himself back through the opening.

Just in time! Four large guard dogs were running to the fence, barking loudly. The noise was terrible. Steve pulled the bag off his head. In the moonlight, he could see their open mouths, their large white teeth. He threw handfuls of sand at them and moved away fast. He was closing the opening when suddenly the large searchlights went on. They lit up the area. Men were shouting and running about.

Steve threw himself onto the ground and moved back into the darkness, away from the searchlights. A group of men was walking along the fence. One of them looked like Big Max. Luckily for Steve, the dogs were running away and were following the men.

Steve moved back to the car. He didn't want to start it yet but he wanted to be prepared.

'Maybe they'll send out cars and search the area around the fence,' he thought. He was lucky – they didn't. After a time, the searchlights went out and all was dark and silent again.

Steve waited for some time in the dark. He listened. He had the feeling that he wasn't alone. Somewhere out there in the darkness, someone was watching him. Maybe he or she was watching him earlier and saw him under the fence of the Blue Mines. Who was it?

Steve got into his car and drove off. No other car followed him. When he passed Liza's dugout, he couldn't see her old red car. Maybe the watcher in the darkness was Liza!

There was still a light in the bar of the hotel. Steve put his head around the door. 'Anyone at home?' he called out.

Sheila was cleaning the bar. She jumped when she heard Steve's voice.

'Hey, what are you doing here? I thought you were in bed.'

'And why aren't *you*?' Steve laughed.

'I can't go to bed yet,' she told him. 'Dad's away in Pimboola. He'll be back soon. Would you like a drink with me, Steve? No need to pay!'

'That's kind of you! Yeah, I would like a beer.'

'Have you been out?' Sheila brought two glasses to one of the tables and sat opposite Steve.

'Yeah. I couldn't sleep. Just went for a drive.'

'You be careful, Steve. I told you that those Blue Mines people are dangerous.'

'I'll be careful.'

'That's what Andy said. You know – the miner that they found dead near the McKenzie Mine. And look what happened to him!'

'Moornie thinks Andy was killed by McKenzie's ghost.'

'You don't really believe that, do you? Why don't you ask Liza? She was Andy's girlfriend, but she's also very friendly with Duvall, the manager of Blue Mines.'

'So you think Liza knows something about Andy's death?' Steve asked quickly.

'Maybe – but I'm not really interested. Andy wasn't my type. But you *are* my type, Steve!' She looked at him with her large green eyes. Sheila's smile was inviting. Steve was pleased when he heard her father's car in front of the hotel. Sheila was a good-looking woman but he wanted to keep his mind on his job!

Chapter 8 Jim Bowman Agrees to Help

When Steve woke up the next morning, he decided to see Liza again. He wanted her to talk. Did Liza kill Andy or did she know his killers? She had to talk to him. He could be very rough when necessary.

At the shop Steve met Jim Bowman, Eddie's friend. Jim looked very angry, but he was pleased to see Steve. 'That terrible Duvall!' He spoke in a loud voice. 'I told him what I thought of him!'

'Good,' said Steve. 'Let's talk about Duvall. What's he done to you?'

'Yeah, let's talk,' Jim agreed. 'But not here. Let's go to your hotel room. I don't want anybody to see me anywhere with you.'

'Thanks!' Steve laughed. 'My room is the third one. Just go in. I'll get some drinks from the bar.'

They sat on Steve's bed. Steve put a sheet in front of the window, and the room was almost dark.

'What about the other rooms?' Jim asked.

'They're empty,' Steve told him.' I checked them just now. I think I'm the only guest. But tell me, what happened?'

'It's Big Max,' Jim said angrily. 'He attacked Eddie again. He hates Aborigines. I told him to stop attacking Eddie, and we started to have a fight. Duvall came and stopped us. And then Duvall got angry with me – not with Max, but with *me*! I said a few things to him which he didn't like. Then he said: "If you fight with Big Max again, I'll throw you out." He doesn't know yet that I want to get out soon. They pay me good money. In about two months, I'll have enough. Then I'll leave.'

'Where to?' Steve asked.

'Adelaide. My dad died. He left me his house. It's an old one and quite small, but it's mine. I want to take Sheila with me.'

'Sheila?' Steve was surprised.

Jim suddenly became shy. 'I – I really like Sheila, you know. And it's no life for a girl like that. She stands behind the bar day and night, pouring out drinks. I want to give her a better life. I want to take her away from all that.'

'Have you told Sheila?'

'Not yet,' Jim told him. 'I'll talk to her when I have enough money.'

'Sheila probably won't like your plans,' Steve thought. But he didn't say anything. He felt that it wasn't his business. He thought hard.

'If I give you the money now,' he suggested, 'you won't have to wait for two months.'

'You have no idea what I earn,' Jim said.

'Well, if I give you four thousand, will that be enough?'

Jim looked hard at Steve. 'What do you want for that?'

'To have a look inside the secret area of the Blue Mines,' Steve repiled.

'Why do you think there *is* a secret area?'

Steve smiled. 'Isn't there? Well, are you going to take me inside?'

'Four thousand! Your magazine must be very rich to pay that kind of money.' Jim gave Steve a searching look.

'There are a few other people who are ready to pay too,' Steve told him.

'Oh, so that's it! I didn't think you were a travel writer. Well, I don't mind who you are. It doesn't matter to me. I want to get my money. How are you going to pay?'

'I'll pay you one thousand now in notes – and the rest after the job, okay?'

'Okay. When do you want to go inside?'

'As soon as possible. What about tonight?'

'That's all right with me.'

'Do you think you can get me in?' Steve asked.

'I think I can. I'll have to hide you in my car under some old clothes. Murphy's the guard tonight. He never checks anyone. I'll have to take you in at about ten. I don't want to be the last one in. You'll have to stay in my car. I'll get you when everybody's gone to sleep. I think I'll go now. I don't want to give them ideas.' Jim got up. 'Thanks for the drink. I'll meet you at quarter to ten behind the shop. Stay in the dark until I come.'

'Hey, don't you want the first thousand?' Steve started to pull hundred dollar notes from his pocket.

'Wow! Do you always carry so much money?' Jim asked, surprised.

'Not always.' Steve laughed. 'Only when I need it.'

Jim wanted to leave, but Steve suddenly pulled him back. 'Wait a minute,' he said. 'We aren't alone.'

The two men watched from the darkness of the room. They saw Liza walking along the back of the building towards her small red car at the corner of the pub.

'Do you think she heard anything?' Jim asked.

'I hope not.' Steve didn't look very pleased. When Liza drove off, he went quickly into the room next to his. The door was open. Was Liza hiding inside the room while they were talking? Maybe she went in after he checked it. Steve remembered that he closed the door. So somebody opened it again! He walked over to the wall nearest to his bedroom and knocked on it. The wall was very thick.

'Okay,' he told Jim. 'I'll see you at quarter to ten tonight.'

Jim left, and Steve drove to the police station. It was locked. Steve opened it with the key from Travers. He walked into Travers' office and switched on the answering machine. He could hear Travers' voice. The message was in the secret language which the police sometimes used. 'I've gone to Pimboola,' the message said. 'Back at eleven tonight.'

Steve used the same secret language and put a message into the machine. 'I'm going into the Blue Mines at about ten tonight,' it said. 'Jim Bowman is going to take me to the secret area.'

Chapter 9 Inside the Secret Tunnel

Jim's car was an old green Ford. It had no back seats. Steve lay down on the floor of the car and covered himself with some old clothes.

Jim was right. Murphy, the guard, didn't check Jim's car and they got inside, onto the Blue Mines' land. Jim parked away from the other cars, closer to the mine shaft. 'I'll leave you now, Steve,' he told his passenger. 'I'll be back when everything's quiet.'

'Okay. Don't fall asleep!' Steve told him.

Steve waited patiently under his cover. He was pleased that it was cooler now than in the daytime. Some more cars were arriving and he could hear loud voices and laughter. Then all was silent. He seemed to wait a long time. Finally, he heard footsteps and Jim's voice. 'Some of them are still playing cards,' Jim told him softly. 'But I don't think they'll worry us.'

'Where are Duvall and Dr Frank?' Steve asked.

'I haven't seen them. But there's a light in Duvall's living room. They're probably both there.'

They walked slowly to the wooden building which was the entrance to the mine. 'What about the dogs?' Steve remembered suddenly.

Jim laughed. 'Two are in the guard building with Murphy. I've given the other two something that will help them sleep.' He opened a little door and they went quietly inside the building. Jim switched on the big lights. They lit up the area. The opening to the shaft was large. There was a metal ladder into the shaft, but there was also a large metal lift. Jim opened the lift door with a special key.

'Has everyone got a key to the lift?' Steve asked.

Jim laughed. 'No, I took Big Max's key when he wasn't looking. I'm very good at that kind of thing.'

The lift stopped at the bottom of the mine. There were big

lights all around the area. It was very bright. Tunnels went off to the right and to the left.

'Come this way.' Jim took Steve's arm and pulled him along. It was a wide tunnel, wider than the others. The walls were smooth and there was no sign of mining.

'Are they mining for opals in this tunnel?' Steve asked.

'No. Only in the others. This is a special one. You'll see.'

The tunnel widened suddenly into a small, round area. The walls of the area were rough. There were holes in one of the walls and piles of small rocks and sandy earth were all over the floor.

'That's all here for the police,' Jim explained. 'Looks like an opal mining area, doesn't it? But watch!' He walked to one of the walls and pushed in a piece of rock. Part of the wall moved to one side and they looked down a long, wide area with lots of doors. Some of the doors were open, and light was shining from them.

'There's someone in there,' Steve said softly. 'All the lights are on.'

'They always have all the lights on down here,' Jim told him. 'Day and night. These are the factory areas and the laboratory.'

'What do they make down here?' Steve asked quickly.

'You'll see.' Jim pushed him into a room on the right. It was full of large brown boxes. 'Look!' he told Steve. 'Everything is packed and ready to go. Tomorrow night we'll put it onto the lorries and take it to a secret airfield. From there, it's flown out of the country.'

'But what is it?' Steve was getting impatient.

'Nerve gas. It was Dr Frank's idea. He's very clever. It's a terrrible gas. It kills all the nerves in your body. And it's painful too. You scream with pain while you're dying.'

'Andy! That's how he died.' Steve's voice was shaking. He was very angry.

'Yeah. I think so. Maybe they tried it on him. Shall we go back?'

'No. I want to have a look at the area where they make the gas. I also want to see the laboratory. You stay here. If they find you here, just tell them a story. You saw someone. He went into the mine and you followed him. Don't worry about me.'

Steve walked softly across the wide area and through one of the open doors. The factory area was full of machines and large metal cans. Steve moved around quietly, taking photos with a small camera. From the factory area, there was a door to a large laboratory. Steve could see tall and small bottles, some gas rings and a lot of other equipment.

'This is the place where Dr Frank does his experiments,' Steve thought. He was going into the laboratory when he heard voices, male voices and one female voice. He threw himself down and moved slowly across the floor. Then he hid under a large table.

At the end of the laboratory was a small office. Steve could see Duvall, the manager of Blue Mines. He was sitting at his desk. Three people were standing round him. One of them was Dr Frank. The other two were Sheila and her father. They were all speaking very loudly. Slowly, Steve moved closer and listened.

'Why won't you do it?' Duvall asked. 'You just need to tell him that you know a way into the mine. You offer to take him inside. We'll do the rest. This isn't the first time that you've done it, Sheila!'

'But that was different.' Steve could hear Sheila's voice, loud and hard. 'That Andy was stupid. "My father's paid by Duvall," I told him, "I really hate Duvall and my father, and I want to get away from them. They're dangerous."' She laughed loudly. 'And he believed me! Steve is cleverer. I can't tell him that story. And don't forget – I want more money.'

'We've already paid you and your father a lot of money for that snake.' Duvall sounded angry.

'Yeah. And that was a terrible job!' Sheila told him. 'It nearly bit dad. And what happened? Nothing. Steve probably thinks that we put it there.'

'Sheila likes Steve.' Sheila's father laughed loudly.

'Oh, be quiet!' Sheila didn't sound very pleased. 'Maybe I do like him a little. But he's from the police, isn't he? And if Duvall pays me a few thousand more, I'll bring him in here.'

'Duvall tells me that you like Jim Bowman,' Dr Frank said in his strange voice. 'We don't trust Bowman. I want to use him for my experiments, but I haven't yet. I don't want to kill your boyfriend, Sheila.'

'Jim Bowman!' Sheila's laugh was hard and unpleasant. 'He's the last man in Arralooma that I want to have as a boyfriend. All right, he's always in the bar. He tells me how much he loves me. And I took the opal that he bought for me. That doesn't mean I like him. Use him for your experiments, Dr Frank! I won't be sad. He'll be out of my way.'

Steve felt cold inside. He wanted to shoot the girl. She put the snake in his bed. She was ready to take him into the mine – to his death – for money. She took Andy to his death. But something really shocked him – and he wasn't often shocked. It was the way that Sheila talked about Jim. She didn't mind if Dr Frank used Jim for his experiments! Dr Frank wanted to try the nerve gas on Jim. He wanted to kill him. Sheila knew what a terrible death this was.

Steve took the gun from his belt. His first bullet was for Sheila. She had to die. But a quick death was really too good for her. Then he stopped himself shooting. He had to get out alive with his important information – his small camera with all the photos. He thought of Jim. A 'one-man war' was dangerous for him too.

Unhappily, Steve pushed his gun back into his pocket and moved slowly and quietly back into the factory area. From there he went into the room where Jim Bowman was waiting impatiently for him.

Chapter 10 The White Fog

Jim looked worried. 'I heard voices,' he told Steve.

'Yeah. That's right. Duvall and Dr Frank are in the small office next to the laboratory and–' Steve didn't really want to continue. 'Sheila and her father are there too.'

'What!' Jim cried. 'They've taken Sheila! I must get her out of here!'

'Wait! Don't be stupid!' Steve held Jim's arm. 'Sheila and her father are working for Duvall.'

'I don't believe it!' Jim was trying to shout, but Steve quickly put his hand over Jim's mouth.

'I listened to them,' Steve told Jim quickly. 'Sheila put a dangerous snake into my bed. She said so. Did Eddie tell you about the snake?'

'Yeah.' Jim's eyes opened wide.

'Sheila brought Andy into the mine so Duvall and Frank could kill him. They wanted her to do the same to me.'

'Her father told her to do it!' Jim spoke quickly. He was breathing hard. 'It was her father. He's like an animal. She's afraid of him!'

'Listen to me!' Steve shook him. 'It was her. She was asking for more money. And that Dr Frank doesn't like you. He wants to use you for his experiments. You know what that means. And she didn't mind. She said so.'

Jim looked very pale. He was shaking. Suddenly he gave a terrible shout, pulled away from Steve and ran out of the room and across into the laboratory. Steve followed.

Sheila and her father were walking through the laboratory towards them. Sheila's eyes opened wide when she saw Jim. Jim ran to her, shouting at her. He took her by the shoulders and started to shake her. Before Sheila's father could help her, Steve knocked him to the floor. Then he looked up. Duvall was standing in the door to the office, a gun in his hand.

Steve threw himself to the floor. 'Be careful!' he shouted to Jim. Jim pushed Sheila against a table. Then he turned to attack Duvall. There were shots, and Jim gave a shout of pain and fell to the floor. Sheila ran to the door, screaming for help. Steve pointed his gun at Duvall and shot him in the leg. Then he jumped up, took Jim by the shoulders and pulled him towards the door. He saw Dr Frank at the back of the laboratory. Frank was running towards the door to the factory.

Above him, Steve could hear voices screaming. He could hear the noise of running feet. He looked towards the mine shaft. They couldn't escape that way. Steve was sure the mine workers were already on their way down. He looked to the other side. At the end he saw an open door and, through it, a long tunnel. There was a light at the end of the tunnel. 'That tunnel must go somewhere,' he thought. 'Maybe another exit from the mine?' He pulled Jim towards the door and through it into the tunnel.

'Not in here! Not in here!' Jim shouted. 'That's the experimental tunnel!'

But it was too late. When Steve turned round, he could see Dr Frank. Frank was running towards the tunnel. In his hand he was holding a long metal can. Steve pointed his gun at Dr Frank, but the strange scientist was quicker. The metal can hit the floor of the tunnel with a loud noise, and the door shut behind them.

Steve pulled Jim up onto his back and tried to run along the tunnel towards the light. It was difficult with a heavy man on his back.

'The nerve gas!' Jim screamed. 'The white fog! It's coming closer! I can't breathe!'

Steve, too, was having problems. The fog started to fill his nose and his mouth. But the light at the end of the tunnel was becoming brighter. He could hear voices. 'Help! Help!' he shouted, coughing out the fog. 'Help!'

'Steve! We're here!' It was Liza's voice. And then Eddie ran towards them. He helped Steve push Jim through an opening at the end of the tunnel. Steve saw that they were in a narrow tunnel. It was very dark. The only light came from Liza's and Moornie's bright miners' lights.

There was no time for talking. Liza helped Steve carry Jim along. Moornie and Eddie closed up the opening as fast as possible with rocks and sand and wet sheets. They didn't want the gas to come through too quickly.

'Where are we?' Steve asked Liza as they moved slowly along the narrow tunnel.

'In the McKenzie Mine. But we can get through to Moornie's mine,' she told him.

They reached a second opening, a little larger than the first one. They pushed Jim through it. When they were all on the other side, Eddie and Moornie again started to close the opening as fast as possible. Steve noticed large cans with water on each side of the opening. They had a lot of old sheets in them. He helped Moornie and Eddie close the opening with rocks and sand. Then they pushed the wet sheets over them.

'Did you know it was a gas?' Steve asked Liza.

'Yes. I was afraid of that. This won't hold it for very long. But it'll give us enough time to get out of the mine.'

She was right. Steve was breathing more easily. The air was clearer. There was no sign yet of the white fog.

They didn't have to go far to the shaft of Moornie's mine. Steve and Eddie were carrying Jim, while Liza and Moornie were guiding them with their lights to the bottom of the shaft. Jim's eyes were closed and he was breathing heavily. There was a lot of blood on the front of his shirt. Liza tied a cloth over his chest. 'We have to get him out of here and to a hospital as quickly as possible,' she told Steve softly. 'He's lost a lot of blood.'

There was no lift in Moornie's mine, just a metal ladder up the side of the shaft. Eddie climbed up and threw some ropes down. They tied them around Jim's body. Then Moornie and Eddie pulled Jim slowly up and out of the mine. Steve followed them up the ladder. He held Jim's body so it didn't hit the sides of the shaft.

The mine shaft came out of the ground not far from Moornie's dugout. Steve could see the entrance to the McKenzie Mine a few hundred metres away, and then the Blue Mines' land. At the Blue Mines, all the large searchlights were on. The area looked bright and unreal – like the inside of a theatre. People were running here and there. Steve could hear shouting and gun shots.

'Police,' Liza explained to Steve. 'When Bill Travers got your message on his answering machine, he radioed for help from Pimboola. He asked them to send men to the mine by plane. I think they've arrived.'

'Good old Bill Travers!' Steve was pleased that the sergeant acted so quickly.

'Eddie's gone to the dugout to get the car,' Moornie told Steve. 'We'll drive Jim to hospital. Don't worry, he'll live.'

'Thanks, Moornie.' Steve took the old man's hand. 'You saved our lives.'

Moornie smiled. 'Thank Liza. She planned it all.'

Steve turned to Liza. She was watching him with an amused smile. He moved very close to her. 'I'm sorry. I feel terrible, you know. I thought you helped kill Andy. When I found his recorder . . .'

'Moornie gave it to me. They left it in Andy's belt, but they took out the cassette.'

'But why did they put the body near the McKenzie Mine?'

'Maybe they were afraid that someone saw Andy go into the Blue Mines. So they decided to leave his body outside the McKenzie Mine.'

'Liza,' Steve gently took her hand, 'I'm so grateful to you for all your help and I have so many questions. Who are you? Why are you doing all this? How did you know?'

Liza smiled at him. 'And I'll be happy to answer them all, Steve, but not tonight. I'm very tired. And there's Eddie with the car. Jim needs your help now.'

'I must talk to you, Liza!'

'Yes. Tomorrow. Good night, Steve!' Liza turned round and walked away into the darkness.

Chapter 11 Liza

A doctor was flown in from Pimboola. He took the bullet out of Jim's chest. 'Jim's going to be okay,' he told Steve. 'But he's lost a lot of blood and needs plenty of rest.'

Steve was waiting in the hospital. He was very tired but he wanted to keep awake. A kind nurse gave him a cup of strong coffee. Then Sergeant Travers walked in. He looked hot and dirty.

'Well, Steve, we've finished the job. We got them all! Duvall, Dr Frank, Sheila and her father. We're flying them to Pimboola prison tonight. We've also got all the miners. They're going to Pimboola for questioning. Of course, when Jim's better, we want to talk to him too. Oh, and Duvall's badly hurt. He's got two bullets in his leg. I think somebody shot at him.' He gave Steve an amused smile.

Steve laughed. 'Thanks a lot, Bill. You acted so quickly when you got my message.'

'That's all right. I was looking for an excuse to get into that place.'

'How *did* you get in?' Steve asked.

'We had to shoot our way in. And those terrible dogs! One of them nearly bit me. But I'm happy now. We found a nerve gas

KING ALFRED'S COLLEGE
LIBRARY

factory, Steve, with a laboratory and everything. Of course, that's why they needed the secret airfield. They were flying it out of the country.'

'Yeah,' Steve agreed. 'A nice little business. Someone was making millions of dollars. But how did you get into the laboratory and factory area? The entrance was well hidden.'

'When we got down there, it was wide open. That girl Sheila was standing at the entrance, shouting for help. She thought we were miners. She wanted us to go into the laboratory and kill you. Then she realized who we were. It's a pity you didn't see the look on her face! I'm really shocked about Sheila. That friendly girl from the hotel bar! She told us a lot of lies. "Duvall brought me into the mines," she told us. "I didn't want to come." That didn't help her. Her father told us everything. And then she screamed at him, calling him all kinds of names!'

'You know, Sheila took Andy into the mine, to his death,' Steve told Travers. 'And she put that snake into my bed.'

'Well, it just shows you – you can't trust women!'

'You can't trust *some* women,' Steve corrected him. 'And you can't trust some men. Sheila's father, for example.'

'Okay, okay,' Travers laughed. 'I agree that there're some nice women – like Liza.'

'I'm surprised, Bill Travers! I thought you didn't trust Liza.'

The sergeant laughed. 'Well, I made a mistake. We all make mistakes sometimes.'

'Bill, who is she and why's she helping us?'

'*She* wants to tell you. Ask her!'

'I will – but I must get a few hours' sleep.'

◆

Steve slept badly. The men from the Pimboola police were searching the hotel. They were laughing and calling out. Early in the morning, he was woken up by Crazy Fred. Fred brought him a cup of tea and quite a good breakfast. Steve was surprised.

'I own part of the hotel, Steve,' Fred told him. 'And I didn't work for the Blue Mines. You must believe me. The police do. I can keep the hotel open. I knew there was something wrong with those Blue Mines people. I didn't know what it was. I didn't, believe me. I talked to Andy about it. Andy didn't tell me much. Andy wasn't a miner – I know that now. He was from the police. And you're from the police too, aren't you, Steve? I'm so pleased I'm your friend!' Crazy Fred laughed, showing his big white teeth. Then he ran out of the room.

It was getting hot outside. Steve had a cold shower and went to see Liza. She looked beautiful in her clean white T-shirt and light grey jeans.

'Hi!' She smiled at him. 'Come in! Have a cup of coffee! I'm just making one.'

Steve sat down and looked at her. 'Who are you? And don't tell me that you're an opal cutter. I won't believe it.'

'But I *am* an opal cutter, Steve. When I was in Amsterdam, I did a course in opal cutting. It's very useful in my job. You need to know a lot of things.'

'And what's your real job?' Steve asked.

Liza laughed. 'The same as yours, Steve. But you're working for the Australian government and I'm working for another country. My country was also getting worried about the Blue Mines. So they sent me here.'

'But why didn't you work with Andy?' Steve asked.

'I tried to. I *thought* Andy was working for the Australian government. I offered to help him. But I think Andy didn't trust me. And I couldn't tell him who I was working for.'

'Andy trusted that terrible Sheila,' Steve said angrily. 'And that's why he died.'

'That was sad. I was in Pimboola when he disappeared. I was so unhappy that I couldn't help him.'

'But the McKenzie Mine and Moornie?' Steve asked.

Liza smiled. 'I was looking for an entrance into the Blue Mines. I thought of an underground entrance. The McKenzie Mine isn't used now, and it's close to the Blue Mines. Then I found that Moornie and Eddie hated the Blue Mines people. Moornie already had an opening from his mine into the McKenzie Mine.

'Why did he make one?'

'Ask him! One of the miners told me about Robert McKenzie. McKenzie always thought there were large opals in his mine. That's why he was making the new tunnel. I think Moornie hoped to find the opals.'

'And he told the ghost stories so people stayed away from the McKenzie Mine?' Steve asked.

'I think so. Well, I paid Moornie enough money to buy the McKenzie Mine. Then Moornie, Eddie and I tried to discover what was happening underground in the Blue Mines. We broke through the wall into Dr Frank's terrible experimental tunnel only yesterday. We found a piece of Andy's belt. It probably broke when they carried him out. I could also smell gas. I told Bill Travers about it when he came back from Pimboola last night. He told me of your plan to go inside the mine with Jim. The most dangerous part down there was the experimental tunnel. So we went down into the mine and prepared to help you. Bill wanted to come with us but he had to wait for the Pimboola police.'

'Liza, you've been great!' Steve touched her hand.

She smiled at him.

Suddenly, Eddie ran into Liza's dugout. Moornie followed more slowly. He carried a little cloth bag.

'Steve, Liza! Look what Uncle found in the McKenzie Mine. We've worked in that new tunnel all morning. They were in the place where Robert McKenzie said. One wall of the tunnel is full of them!'

Moornie opened his little bag. Slowly he took out some large blue uncut opals and put them carefully on the table.

'Moornie! They're beautiful!' Liza shouted. 'And you'll get a lot of money for them.'

The old man smiled. 'For Eddie,' he said. 'I want Eddie to go to college. I'll send Eddie to Adelaide. Jim has a little house there. Eddie can stay with him and go to college.'

Eddie laughed. 'But now we're going to the pub. It'll be free drinks for everyone. Are you coming?'

Steve smiled at him. 'Later, Eddie. I'm just going to help Liza.'

Eddie and Moornie left. Steve turned to Liza. 'I have to drive south after lunch. My plane will take me back to Sydney. Will you come with me?'

Liza shook her head. 'No, thanks. They've made other plans for me. But I'll have a few days' holiday in Sydney before I start my next job.'

'Great! Let's enjoy it. What about dinner tomorrow night?'

'Fine. I'll give you my phone number in Sydney.' Liza wrote her number on a small piece of paper and gave it to him. Steve took it but held her hand in his. When Liza smiled happily, he pulled her closer to him.

ACTIVITIES

Chapters 1–3

Before you read

1 This story happens in Arralooma, in the centre of Australia. What do you know about the centre of Australia? Is it hot or cold? Does it rain a lot? Are there high mountains or low hills? Are there many trees? Is there a lot of sand?

2 Find these words in your dictionary. They are all in the story. Use them in the sentences below.

dugout licence mine opal shaft tunnel

a Many people in Arralooma work underground in the . . . . ..
b They live in . . . . ., not in houses.
c They climb down deep . . . . . on ladders.
d Then they move underground through long . . . . ..
e They go down there to find . . . . ..
f You have to pay for a . . . . . before you take the stones out of the ground.

3 Answer the questions. Find the words in *italics* in your dictionary.

breathe fog ghost manager snake

a Is it easy or difficult to *breathe* in a smoky room?
b Is it easy or difficult to see through *fog*?
c Which is more frightening: a *ghost* or a *snake*? Why?
d Is a *manager* the boss or the boss's assistant?

After you read

4 Discuss these questions. What do you think?

a Who or what killed Andy?
b Who put the snake into Steve's bed?
c Why does Eddie show Steve the secret airfield?

5 What do you think of Arralooma? Would you like to live there? Why (not)?

Chapters 4–7

Before you read

6 Discuss these questions.

- **a** Have you ever been in an underground mine? What was happening down there? What did you see?
- **b** What will happen to Steve when he visits the Blue Mines?

7 Find these words in your dictionary. Put each word with a word below. Why are you putting them together?

bark *bullet* *fence* *sergeant* *trust*

- **a** police
- **b** building
- **c** dog
- **d** friend
- **e** gun

After you read

8 Who are these people? What do you know about them?

- **a** Moornie
- **b** Big Max
- **c** Mr Duvall
- **d** Dr Frank
- **e** Bill Travers
- **f** Crazy Fred

9 Work with another student. Have this conversation.

Student A: You are Big Max. Tell Mr Duvall what happened on the road.

Student B: You are Mr Duvall. Ask questions. Why didn't Max kill Steve?

10 How does Steve feel about

- **a** Sheila?
- **b** Liza?

Chapters 8–11

Before you read

11 How do you think the story will end?

12 Find the words in *italics* in your dictionary. Answer the questions about them.

a Scientists do *experiments*. Why do they do them?

b What can you find in a *laboratory*?

c *Nerves* are parts of our body. What other parts can you name?

d What uses do *ropes* have?

After you read

13 Work with other students. Imagine that you are making a film called *The Mystery of the Blue Mines*. Think about one of these parts of the story.

a In Duvall's office (Duvall, Dr Frank, Sheila and her father)

b The fight in the laboratory (Jim Bowman, Sheila, Steve and Duvall)

c In the Experimental Tunnel, the McKenzie Mine and Moornie's Mine

Make notes on your speeches, your movements and the equipment that you need. Then act it out in front of the class.

Writing

14 You were in the pub when Steve and Big Max fought. Write a letter to a friend. Tell him/her what happened.

15 Write Liza's report to her government about the Blue Mines. Tell them about Andy and Steve.

16 Sheila's father tells Sergeant Travers what he and Sheila did for Duvall. Write the sergeant's report.

17 You are Steve. It is a year later. Write to Liza. What have you done in that year? What are your plans?

Answers for the Activities in this book are published in our free resource packs for teachers, the Penguin Readers Factsheets, or available on a separate sheet. Please write to your local Pearson Education office or to: Marketing Department, Penguin Longman Publishing, 5 Bentinck Street, London W1M 5RN.